This Little Hippo
book belongs to

_____

_____

For Florence, Fintan,
Armon, Evan,
Hannah and Oliver

Scholastic Children's Books,
Commonwealth House, 1-19 New Oxford Street,
London WC1A 1NU, UK
a division of Scholastic Ltd

London • New York • Toronto • Sydney • Auckland
Mexico City • New Delhi • Hong Kong

First published by Little Hippo,
an imprint of Scholastic Ltd, 2000

Copyright © Tracey and Andrew Rogers, 2000

ISBN 0 439 01382 8

Printed in Italy by Amadeus S.p.A. - Rome

Monkey's Surprise

Tracey and Andrew Rogers

Little Hippo

It was a beautiful day in the jungle and Monkey was happy. There was nothing he liked more than relaxing in his hammock with a cold drink and a good book.

But the peace and quiet didn't last long.
"Let's play here," said Crocodile.

"There's plenty of room," said Ostrich.
"Good idea," said Tiger. They began
to play a game.

"Hooray!"
said Ostrich.

"Yippee!"
said Elephant.

"Oops!"
said Crocodile.

"Whack!"
shouted Tiger.

"This is fun!"
said Giraffe.

"Catch it!"
shouted Snake.

Monkey was trying hard to read his book.

THWACK! The ball flew high into the air and landed with a bump on Monkey's head.

"Ouch!" yelled Monkey. "That does it," he said. "I'm going to sort this out." Monkey reached for his telephone and made a call.

Soon the postman arrived with a large parcel.

All the animals crowded round the parcel.
"I wonder what's inside," said Tiger.

'I hope it's a bike,' thought Giraffe.

'I hope it's a boat,' thought Elephant.

'I hope it's a drum,' thought Crocodile.

'I hope it's a kite,' thought Ostrich.

'I hope it's a painting set,' thought Tiger.

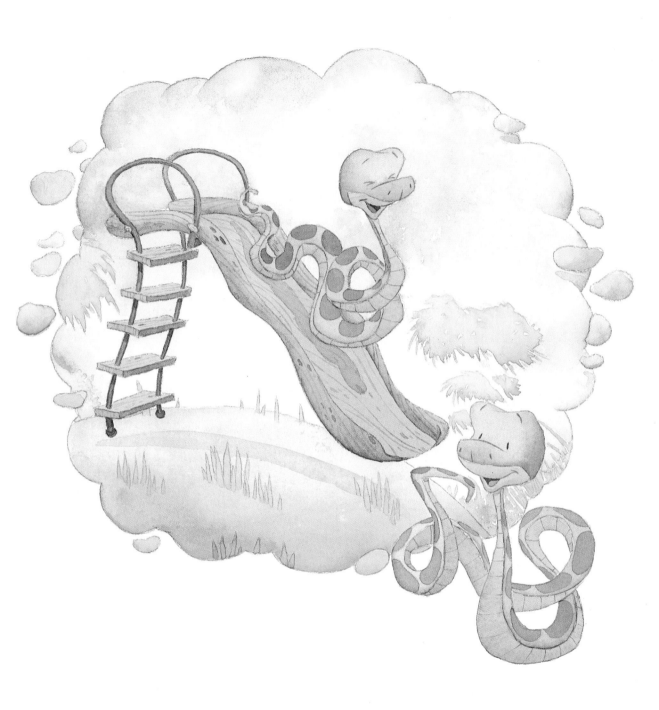

'I hope it's a ssslide,' thought Snake.

Giraffe saw a label on the box.

"It says it's for you, Monkey," she said.

"I was wondering when that would arrive,"
said Monkey.

"What is it?"
asked Ostrich.

"It's a surprise!"
said Monkey.
"It's something
we can all enjoy."

"Open it, open it!"
shouted Tiger
excitedly.

"Hurry up,
pleassse,"
said Snake.

Monkey opened the box and
the animals were surprised and
delighted with what was inside.

"A hot-air balloon!" they shouted.
"Can we have a go?" asked Crocodile.

"Of course," said Monkey. "Climb in."

"Aren't you coming, Monkey?" asked Giraffe.

"I'll have my turn tomorrow," said Monkey.
"Off you go and have a good time."

Waving and smiling, the animals
floated off into the distance.
Monkey was left all alone.

The jungle was quiet again.
"Now I can read my book!" grinned Monkey
and snuggled into his hammock.